Praise for *Toby Wears a Tutu*

"I fell in love with Toby the moment I read this book. Gorgeous illustrations bring Toby's captivating personality to life as they bravely face the challenge to be authentic and honest with their new friends. Toby's mom is another totally inspirational character; no wonder Toby is such an amazing little human. *Toby Wears a Tutu* is a wonderful addition to any child's bookshelf."

—Ellie Royce, author of *Auntie Uncle: Drag Queen Hero*
published by Pow! Kids Books

"This gentle story follows gender non-conforming Toby as they learn how to explain their choices to their new classmates. Brightly colored and warmhearted, this is a wonderful story for young readers."

—Maia Kobabe, author of *Gender Queer: A Memoir*

"*Toby Wears a Tutu* is a heartwarming story about learning to love who you are, regardless of what others might think of you. Even if a child doesn't identify the same way as Toby, all children can relate to Toby's feelings and learn a valuable lesson about appreciating diversity and learning acceptance. As an underrepresented minority in literature, Lori Starling has crafted a beautiful story, showing how loving one's self builds self-esteem and confidence in all children. I would feel extremely comfortable reading this book to my kindergarteners and cannot wait to do so."

—Mary Russell, kindergarten teacher

"*Toby Wears a Tutu* sends a powerful message to children: acceptance. Starling and DuFalla tackle the difficult topic of gender roles with a young person in a whimsical, heartfelt manner that can only be found through the bravery of a child. They invite an important discussion that starts with gender and encapsulates 'othering' experienced by young people. They combine beautiful imagery with powerful words that make *Toby Wears a Tutu* a must for any child's bookshelf."

—Jeremy Flagg, MFA, author, and SNHU creative writing professor

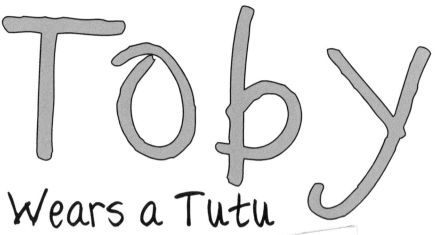

Toby
Wears a Tutu

written by Lori Starling | illustrated by Anita DuFalla

Brandylane
Publishers, Inc.
Publishing books since 1985

ISBN: 978-1-951565-39-8
LCCN: 2020915476

Designed by Michael Hardison
Production managed by Haley Simpkiss

Printed in the United States of America

Published by
Brandylane Publishers, Inc.
5 S. 1st Street
Richmond, Virginia 23219

Brandylane
Publishers, Inc.
Publishing books since 1985

brandylanepublishers.com

*For the child who feels they need
to hide a part of themself to fit in.
This is for you.*

It's the first day of school, and I'm looking my best! With my freshly shaved head, purple glasses, button-down blouse, dapper blue bow tie, and frilly pink tutu, the world is mine to discover!

The first thing we do in class is sit in a circle for reading time. We read a really fun book about bugs and learn how they come in all different shapes and colors. We count the bugs in the book, sing, and clap! It reminds me of the bug hunts I go on with my mom.

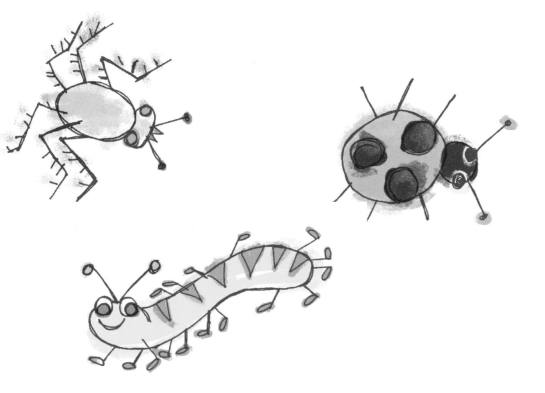

Next, my teacher has us draw pictures of the bugs and other creatures that we see outside every day. I love to draw! I imagine my new class and I are explorers, searching for new plants and animals. In my mind, I am in the rainforest following a giant centipede!

The bell rings. It's time for recess!

I strut to the kickball court, prepared to play.

"You can't play," yells James. "Only boys can play kickball!"

"Wait, what are you?" asks Jessie, pointing at me.

"You look like a boy," giggles Vicki as she jumps rope nearby.

"But he's wearing a frilly skirt! He's a girl!" Marcus laughs.

These questions confuse me and make me nervous.
I go to the tire swing to sit by myself.

At home, I talk to my mom. Mom lets me be my own person. She lets me play football and play dress up in her leopard-print heels. Together, we go on nature hikes and try on different shades of lipstick. We bake cookies and sing karaoke in the living room and dance like no one's watching. She lets me collect bugs, make mud pies, and take karate. She teaches me I can do anything.

Mom reminds me some people think it is important to call myself a girl or a boy, even though it doesn't matter. She says that not everyone will always understand if I do not act like one or the other, so it's important that I talk to my friends about my thoughts and feelings. If I need to, Mom tells me, I can always talk with them in front of an adult I trust, like her or my teacher.

As my mom takes freshly baked cookies out of the oven, she hands me a tube of icing.

"In order to decorate the cookies with the icing, you need to have a strong grip," Mom says. "Just as you grab the bag of icing, you need to grab hold of your courage to speak to your friends. You should always put love into decorating cookies, just as you should put love and kindness into your words."

Mom smiles and shows me how to decorate the cookies. I follow her every move and promise to always grab hold of my courage and speak words of love about myself.

The next day, I see James, Jessie, Vicki, and Marcus again at recess. They come up to me by the tire swing, smiling.

"So, what are you?" asks Vicki.

I stop and stare. I take a deep breath in. I take a deep breath out. My hands shake. I grab the courage that is inside my belly, just like my mom taught me.

I tell them about me. I declare…

"I'm Toby."

"I can EAT anything:

strawberry shortcake, hotdogs with mustard, spinach, collard greens, tacos,

pickles, spaghetti, pizza with anchovies, broccoli, chocolate milkshakes, and even peanut butter and banana sandwiches."

"I can WEAR anything:

basketball shorts, a tuxedo, a sparkly dress, overalls, superhero costumes,

blue blouses, bow ties from my bow tie collection, ballet tights, my mom's bright blue eyeshadow, ruby red lipstick, headbands on my shaved head, and even my pink tutu!"

"I can DO anything:

go puddle jumping and bug hunting, play horseshoes, football, hockey, dodgeball, and princesses, bake cupcakes, master the flute, camp out in the woods in a tent—IN THE DARK—roast marshmallows, and even play kickball!"

"I can BE anything:

a trombone player, a ninja, a police officer, a beauty queen, an opera singer, a ballet dancer, a baker, a soldier, a mechanic, a teacher, a rock star, a racecar driver, a firefighter, and everything in between!"

"Sometimes, I feel like a boy."

"Other times, I feel like a girl."

"But most days, I don't feel like either.

I feel somewhere in between.

I feel like Toby, and it's okay to just be me."

Jessie looks at Vicki. Vicki looks at James. James looks at Marcus.

"So… you're just a Toby?" Marcus asks.

I nod, and then James tugs on my arm. We all run to the kickball court together and play until the bell rings.

It's amazing to just be a me.

About the Author

Lori Starling is a writer, poet, amateur ukulele player, and lover of all things Edgar Allan Poe, Emily Dickinson, and Sylvia Plath. Through their writing, they strive to create realistic worlds for their readers to explore, where marginalized voices are heard and empowered.

Starling holds an MFA in creative writing, as well as a BA in English & creative writing with various associate degrees. In addition to their writing shenanigans on loristarlingwrites.com, their writing can be seen in places like *One Green Planet*, *Life in 10 Minutes Lit Magazine*, and *Beyond Queer Words: A Collection of Poems*. Recently, they have co-founded Clay Literary, which houses two weekly online publications: *FLEDGLING* and *RAVEN*. *Toby Wears a Tutu* is their first children's book.

About the Illustrator

Anita DuFalla is both an award-winning illustrator and designer with fifteen years of experience in children's book illustration.

She sports a collection of more than five hundred patterned pantyhose, and lives in the Friendship neighborhood of Pittsburgh with her son, Lucas.

CPSIA information can be obtained
at www.ICGtesting.com
Printed in the USA
LVHW070225090121
676101LV00015B/1868